1 hunter

by PAT HUTCHINS

Greenwillow Books, New York

For Harry—Number One

10 9 8 7 6 5

Library of Congress
Cataloging in Publication Data

Hutchins, Pat (date)   1 hunter.
Summary: One hunter walks through the
forest observed first by two elephants,
then by three giraffes, etc.
1. Counting—Juvenile literature.
[1. Counting. 2. Animals—Fiction]
I. Title.
QA113.H87   513'.2 [E]   81-6352
ISBN 0-688-00614-0   AACR2
ISBN 0-688-00615-9 (lib. bdg.)

1 hunter

2 elephants

3 giraffes

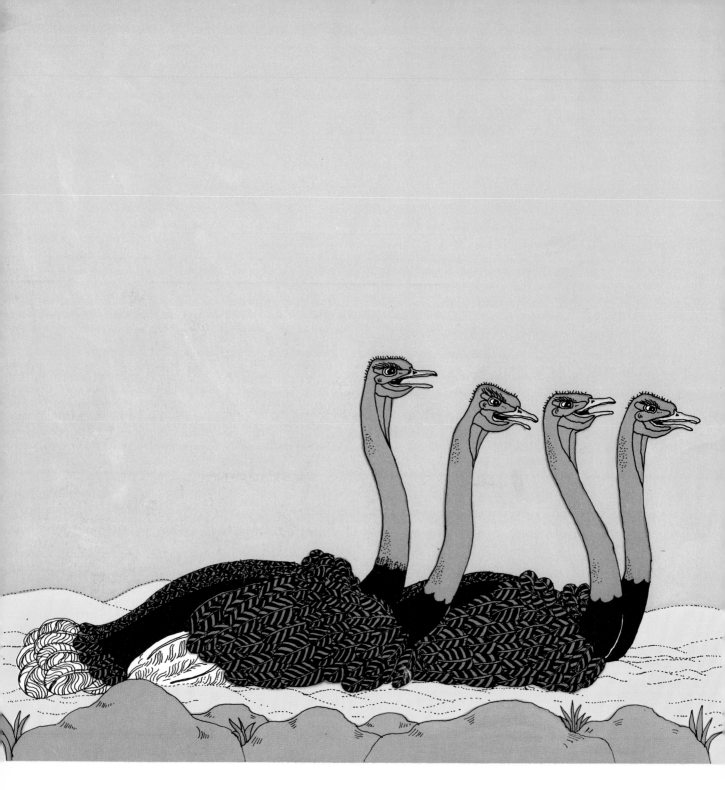

4 ostriches

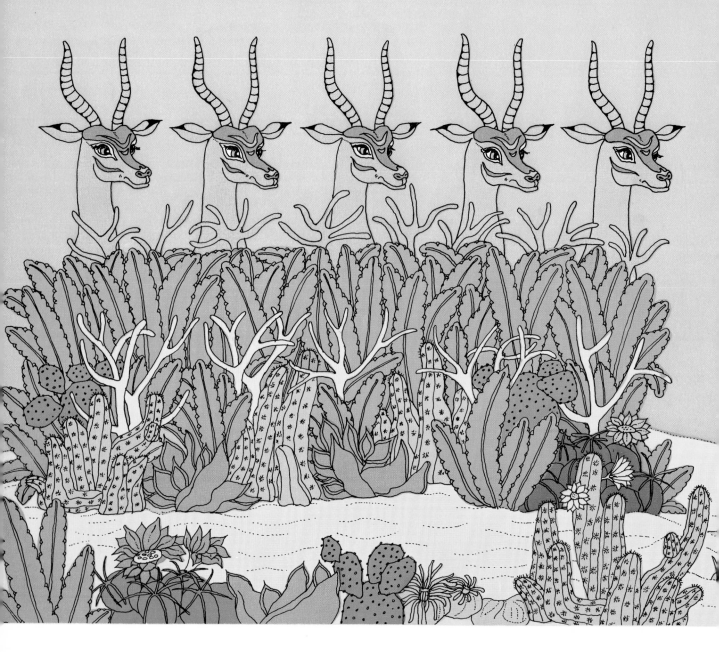

5 antelopes

6 tigers

7 crocodiles

8 monkeys

 snakes

10 parrots

10 parrots   **9** snakes   **8** monkeys
7 crocodiles   **6** tigers   **5** antelopes

4 ostriches 3 giraffes 2 elephants

and 1 hunter